Little Tigers

JO WEAVER

PEACHTREE
ATLANTA

Dawn was breaking in the jungle.

Two little tigers, Puli and Sera, were excited to start their day. But Mother Tiger was worried. Last night, she heard men and dogs on the jungle paths near their home. It wasn't safe anymore.

"My little ones," she said, "we need to find a new home."

"I know somewhere safe," said Sera.

"Then show us the way," said Mother Tiger,
and they all left their den for the last time.

Sera led them away from the danger, through the chattering jungle to where the river plunged over a cliff.

"Over here!" she said, and they leapt
behind the rushing water.

On the other side of the waterfall was a cool, damp cave. Little beads of water glistened on their fur.

"Isn't it lovely!" said Sera.

"Lovely for a frog, maybe," said Mother Tiger kindly. "But too wet for tigers. We need somewhere warm and dry."

"Then I know just the spot!" said Puli.
"Follow me!" he called, leaping into a tree
and scrambling up the branches.

Up and up, the three tigers climbed,
high into the jungle canopy.

"Look how warm and dry it is!" said Puli.

"Yes," agreed Mother Tiger, "and it might be good for
monkeys. But it's a very long way to fall for a tiger. We
need to sleep on the ground. Let's keep looking."

Together they roamed the deepest parts of the jungle, exploring its secret places. Mother Tiger was growing more anxious. The day was passing, and they still hadn't found a new home.

Puli spotted a cave in the rocks.
"What about here?" he asked.
"This looks perfect."

But inside it was full of stinging, biting, creepy crawlies.

"Perfect for insects," sighed Mother Tiger. "But not for us."

So they set off again, still searching for somewhere safe.

"It's lovely and sheltered in here," said Sera, looking under the roots of an old tree.

But a big python slithered from the branches.

The tigers slunk away.

The night was drawing in, and still they had nowhere safe to sleep.
Mother Tiger was very worried.

Then she remembered. There was one place where no one would
find them…

It was somewhere close by, but could she find it before the sun set?

"Wait here, little ones," said Mother Tiger.
She gave them a loving nuzzle and disappeared
into the shadows.

"Will she come back soon?"
whispered Puli.

"I hope so," said Sera, huddling
close to her brother.

At last, they heard their mother's voice.

"Up here," she called. "Don't be scared."

The cubs followed her up a crumbling
staircase and into an old stone temple
overgrown with vines.

Inside, it was warm and dry and safe.
"Our own secret den!" said Sera.

"And we can see the stars!" said Puli, curling up next to his sister.

Mother Tiger watched over them, listening to the familiar sounds of the jungle in the night.

"Good night, my little ones," she whispered.
"Welcome to your new home."

But Sera and Puli were already fast asleep.

For Rowan and Felix,
with all my love. X

Bengal tigers are an endangered species. They live in the Indian subcontinent and are threatened by habitat loss, by conflict with humans, and by poaching for illegal wildlife trade. There are thought to be around only 2,500 Bengal tigers left in the wild today.

FOR FURTHER STUDY VISIT

National Geographic
www.nationalgeographic.com/animals/mammals/b/bengal-tiger

South Asia Wildlife Enforcement Network
www.sawen.org

Wildlife Protection Society of India
www.wpsi-india.org/tiger

Ω

Published by
PEACHTREE PUBLISHING COMPANY INC.
1700 Chattahoochee Avenue
Atlanta, Georgia 30318-2112
www.peachtree-online.com

Text and illustrations © 2019 by Jo Weaver

First published in Great Britain in 2019 by Hodder Children's Books
First United States edition published in 2019 by Peachtree Publishing Company Inc.

The illustrations were rendered in charcoal and digitally colored.

Printed in China
10 9 8 7 6 5 4 3 2 1 (hardcover)
10 9 8 7 6 5 4 3 2 1 (trade paperback)
First Edition

HC ISBN: 978-1-68263-110-2
PB ISBN: 978-1-68263-134-8

Library of Congress Cataloging-in-Publication Data

Names: Weaver, Jo (Children's author), author, illustrator.
Title: Little tigers / written and illustrated by Jo Weaver.
Description: First edition. | Atlanta : Peachtree Publishing Company Inc., 2019. | Summary: Follows a mother tiger and her cubs, Sera and Puli, as they seek a new home away from the men and dogs hunting near their den.
Identifiers: LCCN 2018052682 | ISBN 9781682631102
Subjects: LCSH: Tiger—Juvenile fiction. | CYAC: Tiger—Fiction. | Habitat (Ecology)—Fiction. | Jungles—Fiction.
Classification: LCC PZ10.3.W353 Lk 2019 | DDC [E]—dc23
LC record available at *https://lccn.loc.gov/2018052682*